HAL
and the
VERY LONG RACE

By Lucy Bell

Illustrated by Michael Garton

Written by Lucy Bell
Designed by Tim Palin Creative
Illustrated by Michael Garton

Library of Congress Cataloging-in-Publication Data

Names: Bell, Lucy J., author. | Garton, Michael, illustrator.
Title: Hal and the very long race / by Lucy Bell ; illustrated by Michael
  Garton.
Description: First edition. | Minneapolis, MN : Sparkhouse Family, 2017. |
  Summary: Hal is invited to race with his friends, but with his short legs
  and slow speed, he worries that he is not good enough to keep up.
Identifiers: LCCN 2016037151 | ISBN 9781506417899 (hardcover)
Subjects: | CYAC: Self-confidence--Fiction. | Running--Fiction. |
  Friendship--Fiction. | Christian life--Fiction.
Classification: LCC PZ7.1.B4523 Hal 2017 | DDC [E]--dc23
LC record available at https://lccn.loc.gov/2016037151

First edition published 2017
Printed in United States
22 21 20 19 18 17   1 2 3 4 5 6 7 8

VN0004589; 9781506417899; JAN2017

SPARK
HOUSE
FAMILY
sparkhouse.org

One morning, Hal came out of his hedgehog hole and stretched his arms as far as they could reach into the fresh air.

What a beautiful day! he thought. *I wonder what my friends are doing.*

He went to look for them.

Hal came to the top of a hill and
saw Ava, Rufus, Jo, and Uri.

"Good morning, Hal!" Ava called. "I was just telling the others about my idea for something fun to do. Oh, it's the best, most wonderful idea ever!"

"What is it, Ava?" Hal asked. "A picnic? Hide-and-seek? Skipping rocks in the stream?"

"Even better," Ava said. "We're going to have a race from here to the tree on the other side of the hill!"

Hal's stomach felt like it had dropped
to his toes. This was not good news.

My legs are so short, Hal thought.
I can't go as fast as the others. I'll lose.
Everyone will laugh at me.

Hal didn't want to be alone.
He wanted to spend time with his friends.
And that meant running in the race.

"What do you say, Hal?" Ava asked. "Will you race with us?"

"Um . . . okay," Hal said, "I guess."

Uri flew away with a ribbon for the finish line in her beak.

Ava, Hal, Jo, and Rufus
lined up for the race.

"Okay!" Ava said.
"On your marks . . . get set . . . go!"

Ava, Jo, and Rufus burst forward. Ava and Jo bounded up the hill. Rufus's legs moved so quickly they turned into a blur.

Hal ran as quickly as he could, but his legs couldn't carry him fast enough. By the time he was halfway up the hill, his friends were already on the other side.

Oh no, Hal thought. *This is exactly what I was afraid would happen.* Hal stopped and thought about what to do.

*Maybe I can run just a little bit faster.
I'll still lose—but maybe if I don't lose so
badly, my friends won't laugh at me.*

Hal pushed himself as fast as his legs would carry him. He ran faster than he ever had before, faster than he ever thought he could—then he ran a little bit faster than that.

Finally, he got to the top of the hill, only to find that Ava, Jo, and Rufus were almost at the finish line.

Hal wanted to disappear. He wanted to hide. So he did what he always did when he was feeling embarrassed.

He curled up into a little ball.

As he tucked himself up tight, he
said a prayer to help him feel better.

Dear God,

*I'm not good at doing some things. Please
help me be proud of the things I am good at.*

Amen.

While his eyes were still closed, Hal
felt himself begin to roll down the
hill. He rolled faster and faster.

Hal rolled so fast he couldn't see anything.
But he heard Uri's voice, clear and loud.

"Hal! Hal is *fast*! Go, Hal! Go!"

Hal rolled to the bottom of the hill. When he came to a stop, he uncurled and shook his head, feeling dizzy. His friends all ran toward him.

"Hal!" Ava yelled. "You were so fast!"

"What happened?" Hal asked.

"You came in second!" Ava said. "I was first—but Jo and Rufus were slowing down because they were tired, and you rolled right past them!"

Hal could hardly believe it.

He didn't embarrass himself.
He did his best and it was enough.

"I didn't know you could do that, Hal," Ava said.

Hal stood up straight and tall—as tall as his little legs could make him.

"I might not be very good at running, but I'm great at rolling!"

ABOUT THE STORY

Hal is invited to race with his friends, but he's self-concious about his short legs and slow speed. Will his friends laugh at him? Will he even finish the race? A prayer about gifts helps Hal figure out what he's truly good at.

DELIGHT IN READING TOGETHER

As you read this story, ask your child questions about how Hal might be feeling in different parts of the story. Use this as an opportunity to encourage your child and remind them that they have special strengths too!

ABOUT YOUNG CHILDREN AND PATIENCE

Every child develops at their own pace. If you start to worry that your child may not be measuring up, this story can be a good reminder that every child has unique strengths worth celebrating.

A FAITH TOUCH

God created each person to be unique and wonderful! Sometimes even our shortcomings can reveal our greatest strengths. God loves us just the way we are!

For you created my inmost being; you knit me together in my mother's womb. I praise you because I am fearfully and wonderfully made; your works are wonderful, I know that full well.

Psalm 139:13-14

SAY A PRAYER

Say this prayer Hal said when he felt unsure of himself.

Dear God, I'm not good at doing some things. Please help me be proud of the things I am good at.

Amen.